REMEMBER *the* ALAMO!

by Cynthia Mercati

Perfection Learning®

About the Author

Cynthia Mercati is a writer and a professional actress. She has written many plays for a children's theatre that tours and performs at various schools. She also appears in many of the plays herself.

Ms. Mercati loves reading about history and visiting historical places. When she writes a historical play or book, she wants her readers to feel like they are actually living the story.

Ms. Mercati also loves baseball. Her favorite team is the Chicago White Sox. She grew up in Chicago, Illinois, but she now lives in Des Moines, Iowa. Ms. Mercati has two children and one dog.

Illustrations by Margaret Sanfilippo: cover, pp. 4, 10, 31, 35, 38, 44. Inside Illustration: Mike Aspengren, Kay Ewald

Image Credits: Prints and Photographs Collection, CN 01549, The Center for American History, University of Texas at Austin p. 25

Art Today pp. 3, 7, 8, 9, 11, 12, 13, 14, 17, 18 (lower left), 19 (bottom), 20, 21, 22, 23, 29, 30, 32, 33, 39, 47, 48, 49 (top); Corel pp. 6, 53, 54, 56; Dover Publications pp. 18 (top), 46; Dover Publications, courtesy Texas State Library p. 18 (lower right); Library of Congress pp. 15, 19 (top), 26, 27, 28, 36–37, 45, 49 (bottom), 50, 51, 52

For information, contact
Perfection Learning® Corporation,
1000 North Second Avenue, P.O. Box 500,
Logan, Iowa 51546-0500
Phone: 1-800-831-4190 • Fax: 1-800-543-2745
perfectionlearning.com

Paperback ISBN 0-7891-5043-3
Cover Craft® ISBN 0-7807-9007-3
4 5 6 7 8 9 PP 09 08 07 06 05 04

TABLE OF CONTENTS

FREE LAND

CHAPTER ONE

MY NAME IS Addy McCloud. I used to live on a farm in Tennessee with my ma and pa. When I was ten years old, my ma died from a fever.

Pa was very sad. He wanted a new life. I did too.

So we sold our farm and our house. We sold most of our belongings. What we had left, we put in a covered wagon. Then we started out for Texas.

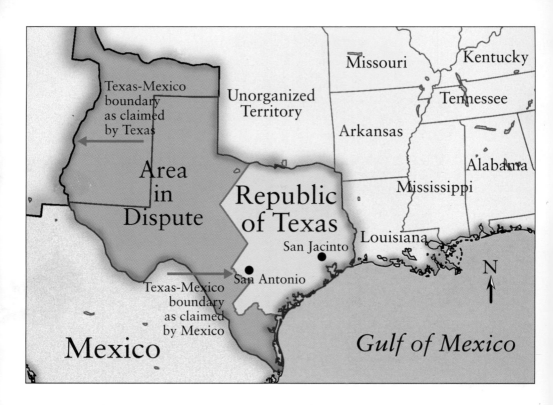

I didn't know anything about Texas. So I asked Pa about it.

"Texas is part of Mexico," he told me. "It has mountains and deserts. But it

doesn't have many people."

"Then how come we're going there?" I asked.

"Texas is a good place. Especially for people who want to start over," Pa answered. "Like us!"

Pa said that a man named Stephen Austin had moved from Arkansas to Texas. He thought it was a great place to live.

The Mexican government wanted more people to settle there. Mr. Austin knew this. So he came up with a plan.

He told the Mexican leaders that Americans would move to Texas if they could get free land. These people would build houses and schools. They would make Texas a safe place to live.

The leaders thought Mr. Austin had a good idea. So they promised 4,000 acres of free land to any American who came to Texas.

"Are we going to get some free land?" I asked Pa. He gave me a big smile.

"You bet we are!"

A BROKEN PROMISE

CHAPTER TWO

PA TALKED ABOUT a time before the white people came. Texas had belonged to the Caddo Indians. They called themselves *Tejas*. *Tejas* was the Caddo word for "friends."

Then Spanish explorers came to Mexico. They turned the word *Tejas* into "Texas."

"Spain once owned Mexico," Pa said. "But in 1821, Mexico fought a war against Spain. The people wanted to be free of Spanish rule."

Pa and I traveled many weeks in our covered wagon. Finally, we got to Texas. Right away, I saw how different it was from Tennessee!

The air was warm and dry. The land was brown. The prairie grass was as tall as Pa!

Pa and I got our free land. It was a few miles outside the town of San Antonio. San Antonio was the capital of Texas. It was named for the river flowing near the town.

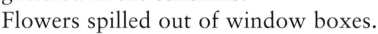

San Antonio was an exciting, noisy place! Many of the buildings were made of white stone. They glittered in the sunshine. Flowers spilled out of window boxes.

People drove little two-wheeled donkey

carts through the streets. Chickens and goats ran everywhere.

The women and girls wore ruffled skirts. They wore colorful shawls over their blouses. The men wore multicolored **serapes** over their white shirts.

Loud, happy music could be heard from **cantinas**.

There were several **mission** churches in the city. Each one had a tall bell tower. One of the churches was called the Alamo.

Pa and I didn't spend much time in San Antonio. We were busy on our farm. We worked from sunup to sundown.

Pa built a cabin out of **adobe**. We decided to raise cotton. Some of the other farmers raised longhorn cattle.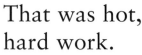

Every September, we had to pick the cotton. That was hot, hard work.

But we didn't always work. Sometimes, we had company over. Then Pa would get out his fiddle and play a tune. My favorite was "Turkey in the Straw."

Pretty soon, everyone would be dancing! We called those parties **fandangos**.

By 1833, some 30,000 Americans lived in Texas. Pa and I had been there for three years.

Pa said there was enough room in Texas for a man to really spread out! I felt the same way!

I loved the wide, open spaces. I loved the sound of the whippoorwills.

I especially loved the wildflowers that bloomed in the spring. I loved to pick them. My favorite flowers were the big yellow roses.

The Americans tried to be good citizens of Mexico. That's what we'd promised the Mexican government. And the Mexican leaders had promised us we could live in freedom.

For a while, they kept their promise. But then a man named Antonio López de Santa Anna took over Mexico. From that time on, everything changed.

SANTA ANNA

CHAPTER THREE

"SANTA ANNA IS a general," Pa said. "He has made himself president of Mexico.

"Before Santa Anna," Pa continued, "the people of Mexico elected their own leaders. They made their own laws. Just like in the United States.

"But Santa Anna threw out the Mexican constitution. He changed laws. He acts like a king!" Pa declared.

Pa got very angry talking about General Santa Anna. His face turned bright red.

"Santa Anna says Americans don't belong in Mexico!" Pa said. "He wants all of us to leave!"

"But this is our land," I exclaimed. I was angry at General Santa Anna now! "We're happy here. I don't want to live anywhere else!"

"Don't worry," Pa said. "Mr. Austin went to Mexico City. That's the capital of Mexico."

Pa explained further. "Mr. Austin is going to see Santa Anna. He's going to ask that Texas be separate from the rest of Mexico. Then we can stay here. We can live the way we want to."

I thought Mr. Austin would be able to change Santa Anna's mind. But I was wrong.

Santa Anna just became angrier at Americans. He put Mr. Austin in jail!

Santa Anna said no more Americans would be allowed to come to Texas. He sent soldiers to Texas. He wanted to make sure his rules were followed.

Pa and I still had company over. But we didn't dance. Now we talked about the general. And we talked about all the bad things he was doing.

After two years, Santa Anna let Mr. Austin out of jail. He came home to Texas. Everyone was glad to see him!

Mr. Austin said that we could never have a good life in Mexico. We could not live under Santa Anna's laws. Everyone in Texas agreed.

On September 19, 1835, Mr. Austin sent a letter to the people of Texas. In the letter, he wrote that we had to go to war against Santa Anna. It was the only way we could make Texas free.

WAR!

CHAPTER FOUR

THE TEXANS DECIDED to fight Santa Anna. They formed their own government.

Henry Smith was elected governor. Sam Houston was made head of the Regular Texas Army.

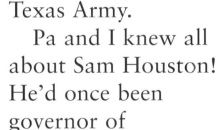

Pa and I knew all about Sam Houston! He'd once been governor of Tennessee!

Texas had a regular army. Plus, there were many small groups of volunteer soldiers. One of those groups was led by William Travis.

Sam Houston

Mr. Travis had been a lawyer and a schoolteacher before moving to Texas. Pa told me that everyone called Mr. Travis "Buck."

Jim Bowie was another man who had moved to Texas. He had his own group of soldiers too. Mr. Bowie had been a scout and a soldier.

He had also invented a new kind of knife. This knife had a special shape. It also had a hand guard for protection. It came to be called a *bowie knife*.

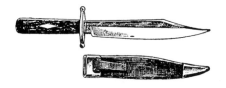

Very soon, the Texans were winning many battles. They drove the Mexican troops out of many towns.

There was a big battle in San Antonio. From our farm, Pa and I could hear the roar of the cannons. With each boom, I jumped.

The Texans won the battle. The Mexican soldiers had to leave San Antonio.

Santa Anna heard that his soldiers were being defeated. He was very angry.

"The Texans have gone too far," Santa Anna said. "Now I am going to crush them!"

Santa Anna would lead the army himself. He would lead the march to Texas.

San Antonio stood right in his path. He would march right through the city.

Many Americans heard Santa Anna was on his way. They quickly left San Antonio.

Some of them stopped at our farm as they passed. They told us the news.

"Jim Bowie, Buck Travis, and their soldiers are in San Antonio," one man told us. "They're going to wait there to fight Santa Anna. They're using the Alamo as their fort."

"Are we going to leave Texas too?" I asked Pa.

"Is that what you want to do, Addy?" Pa asked me.

I shook my head. "No! This is our country!"

"Tomorrow we'll go to San Antonio," Pa said. "I'll tell Mr. Travis and Mr. Bowie that I want to be one of their volunteers. I want to help fight against Santa Anna."

So that's what we did. We packed some food and put it in our wagon. Then we headed for San Antonio and the Alamo. Pa said that when the war was over, Texas would be free. Then we'd move back to our farm. I hoped it would be soon.

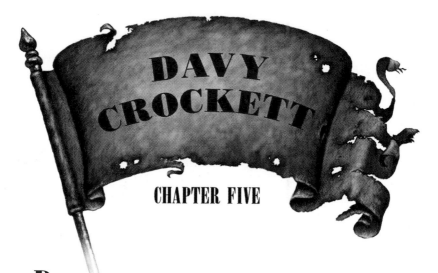

PA SAID THAT the Alamo had been built a long time ago. It was built by Spanish **missionaries**. They called it the Alamo because it was built in a grove of cottonwood trees.

Alamo is the Spanish word for "cottonwood."

A thick stone wall ran all around the Alamo. Inside was a long yard, or **plaza**.

The missionaries had put up several buildings inside the plaza. Most of  them had crumbled into ruins. But the convent was still standing. That was where the missionaries had lived.

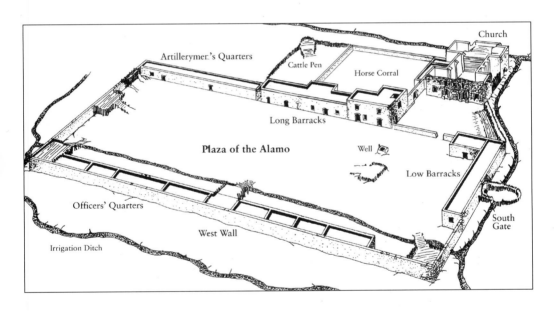

The soldiers had turned the convent into a **barracks**. That's where the soldiers slept. They called it the Long Barrack. They made the second floor of the Long Barracks into a hospital.

There were about 175 men at the Alamo. Many of them had come with Buck Travis or Jim Bowie.

But 32 of them had come on their own. They were men like Pa.

Some of the men at the Alamo had lived far away once. They had moved from Pennsylvania and Massachusetts to Texas.

Not all the Texans in the Alamo were American. Some were Mexicans who thought Santa Anna was a bad leader. They wanted to fight against him too.

One of these men was Gregorio Esparza. He had brought his wife and four children with him.

Almeron Dickinson was a blacksmith. He had moved from Tennessee to Gonzales, Texas. He had come with his wife, Susanna. They had brought their daughter, Elizabeth Angelina.

Everyone called her Angelina. She was 15 months old.

Susanna and I became friends right away. I helped her take care of little Angelina.

Susanna Dickinson

There were several other women at the Alamo. They were sisters or wives of soldiers. The women and children stayed together in the chapel. We fixed food for the men. The meals weren't very fancy. Mostly we just ate **tortillas** and dried beans.

I told Susanna how frightened I was of Santa Anna. I was also afraid of the big army he was leading to San Antonio.

"I'm frightened too," she said. "But we can't let it show. We have to help the men. We have to keep their courage up."

"I'll try to be brave, Susanna," I told her. But I knew it was going to be hard.

On February 8, Davy Crockett arrived at the Alamo!

Mr. Crockett was the most famous frontiersman in the country! He had been a scout and a bear hunter. He had also been a congressman from Tennessee for three terms! He was happy to hear that Pa, the Dickinsons, and I were from Tennessee. He shook our hands.

Vol. I. "Go Ahead!" No. 3.

Davy Crockett's
18 ALMANACK, 37
OF WILD SPORTS IN THE WEST,
Life in the Backwoods, & Sketches of Texas.

O KENTUCKY! THE HUNTERS OF KENTUCKY!!!
Nashville, Tennessee. Published by the heirs of Col. Crockett.

"I'm sure glad to meet you," he said.

Mr. Crockett loved to tell stories. *Tall tales* he called them. He was fun to listen to.

He was fun to look at too. He wore clothes made out of buckskin. He wore a coonskin cap. The tail hung down his back. He had named his rifle "Old Betsy."

We had a big party to welcome Mr. Crockett to the Alamo. He spoke to the crowd. He told us that he had come to Texas to help us fight for our liberty! He'd brought 14 men with him.

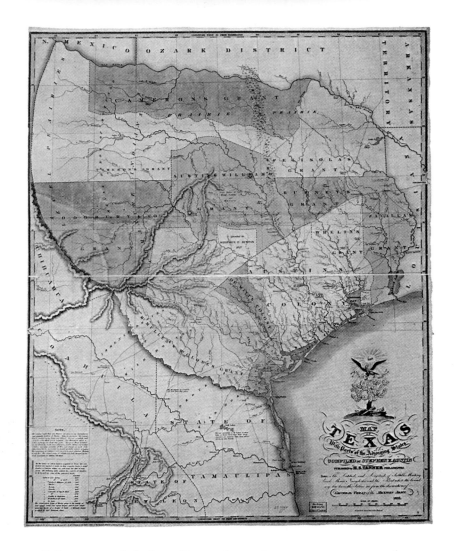

None of Mr. Crockett's men owned any land in Texas. But they'd come to the Alamo. They would help us fight for our rights against Santa Anna.

Mr. Crockett and his men gave me new courage. Pa felt the same way.

"I'm sure glad Davy Crockett is with us," Pa said. "He's a good man to have on your side in a fight!"

A LINE IN THE SAND

CHAPTER SIX

JIM BOWIE HAD ordered a soldier to watch for Santa Anna's army. The soldier stood in the tall tower of the San Fernando church in San Antonio.

On the morning of February 23, 1836, the church bell rang. Everyone in the Alamo knew what that meant. It was a signal. Santa Anna's army was marching into San Antonio.

Shortly after that, Santa Anna raised a red flag from the tower of the same church. Pa and I stood together on the wall of the Alamo. We stared at the flag.

"The red flag means Santa Anna will show us no mercy," Pa said.

Just then, one of Santa Anna's officers rode into the Alamo. He delivered a message to Buck Travis and Jim Bowie. "General Santa Anna demands your surrender!"

Mr. Travis ordered the Alamo's 18-pound cannon to fire one round. That was his answer to Santa Anna. It meant no surrender!

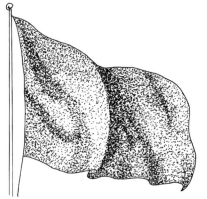

"Victory or death!" Buck Travis shouted.

Santa Anna ordered his men to surround the Alamo. Day and night, they fired their cannons at the wall.

Every day, Santa Anna's soldiers dug deep trenches to hide in. Each new trench was closer than the one before.

Soon the soldiers were so close, we could see the white and blue of their uniforms shining in the sun.

Mr. Travis and Mr. Bowie ordered our men to stand guard on the wall.

Several times, Santa Anna's soldiers rushed toward the Alamo. They fired their rifles at our men. Each time our men drove them back.

All the men inside the Alamo were good shots, especially Davy Crockett! Pa told me he was the finest rifle shot in the world! Pa said Mr. Crockett could shoot the string on a kite in half when it was flying in a high wind!

Our men couldn't sleep. They had to stand on the walls. They had to fight back Santa Anna's men.

The Texans grew very tired. They were running low on ammunition. We were running out of food too.

Jim Bowie had injured his leg. Then the weather turned cold. Mr. Bowie caught **pneumonia**. He was so sick. He had to lie on a cot in the Long Barracks. Buck Travis took over command of all the men. Everyone's spirits had sunk very low.

Then one night, Davy Crockett took out his fiddle. Pa took out his fiddle too. A man named John McGregor took out his bagpipe. Together the men played a tune. Everyone in the Long Barracks clapped. The men on the walls clapped too.

Susanna and I each took one of Angelina's hands. We began whirling her around. Soon *Senora* Esparza and her children were dancing.

"This will show old Santa Anna he can't keep us down!" Pa shouted. We all tried to be brave.

Buck Travis called everyone in the Alamo together. He told us that Santa Anna had 4,000 soldiers. Our men would never be able to defeat an army so large.

Mr. Travis gave all the men a choice. They could stay at the Alamo or escape. He drew a line in the sand with his sword. He said, "Those prepared to give their lives in freedom's cause, cross over to me."

Almost all 189 men stepped over the line. Only one man decided to leave the Alamo.

Mr. Bowie even asked to have his cot carried over the line. I was so proud of Pa when he stepped over the line to stand by Mr. Travis!

Pa held me by the shoulders. He looked deep into my eyes. "Addy," he said, "I want you to remember why we're here. No matter what happens to me. It's like Mr. Travis said. We're fighting for freedom. Just like Americans fought for their freedom from the British back in 1776."

"I'll remember, Pa," I told him. I didn't know those words would be our last.

THE BATTLE

SANTA ANNA'S ARMY had arrived 13 days earlier. It was March 6, five o'clock in the morning. I woke up to the sound of a bugle. It was coming from

Santa Anna's camp. I heard Buck Travis cry out. "The Mexicans are upon us!"

The battle had begun.

My heart started pounding. My eyes got big. I was very scared.

Susanna and I rushed out into the plaza. *Senora* Esparza ran out too. The sky was just turning light.

We heard the thunder of the Mexican cannons. We heard the sound of ladders being flung against the wall. Santa Anna's men were using the ladders to climb over the wall and into the Alamo. We heard the crack of rifle shots.

Mr. Crockett told us to go to a small room next to the chapel. It was called the **sacristy**. He said it was the safest place in the Alamo. The women and children did what Mr. Crockett told us.

We huddled together. Susanna held Angelina tightly in her arms. *Senora* Esparza's four children clung to her skirts. We could hear the sounds of the battle all around us.

Almeron Dickinson ran into the sacristy. His face and arms were stained with gunpowder. He told us that Santa Anna's cannons had blasted a hole in the north wall. Mexican soldiers were pouring in.

"Two times, our men have forced back Santa Anna's soldiers," Mr. Dickinson said.

"But it's hopeless!" he continued. "There are too many of them! More and more are coming all the time. We're almost out of ammunition."

Mr. Dickinson grabbed his wife's hand. "Take care of our daughter," he said. He turned to me. "Addy, your father said to tell you that he loves you."

Mr. Dickinson ran back to join the battle. The women looked at each other. Some of us cried. *Senora* Esparza prayed. All of us were afraid for our men and for ourselves.

All at once, there were no more rifle shots. The cannons were silent. From outside, we heard the Mexican soldiers cheering. They said, *"Viva Santa Anna! Viva Santa Anna!"*

Long live Santa Anna! We knew then that the battle was over. We had lost.

A MEETING WITH SANTA ANNA

CHAPTER EIGHT

THE BATTLE FOR the Alamo had lasted less than two hours.

Our men had fought from the plaza to the Long Barracks. They went in one room and out another.

When they ran out of ammunition, they'd fought with sticks and knives. They'd even fought with their fists. When he could no longer fire his rifle, Davy Crockett swung it like a club.

One of Santa Anna's officers found us. He said Santa Anna would not hurt us. He ordered us to march through the plaza. We saw bodies lying everywhere.

All 188 of our men had been killed.

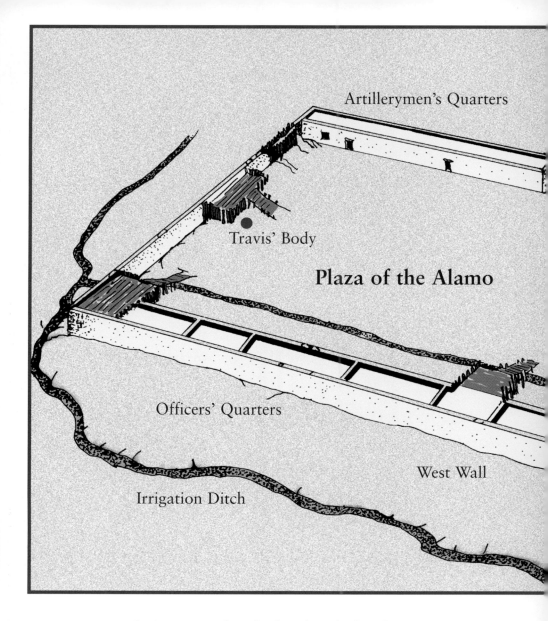

Artillerymen's Quarters

Travis' Body

Plaza of the Alamo

Officers' Quarters

West Wall

Irrigation Ditch

Buck Travis had died while firing a cannon. Jim Bowie had been shot as he lay on his cot. He had been too weak to stand. My pa had died while on the wall. Davy Crockett's coonskin cap lay beside his lifeless body.

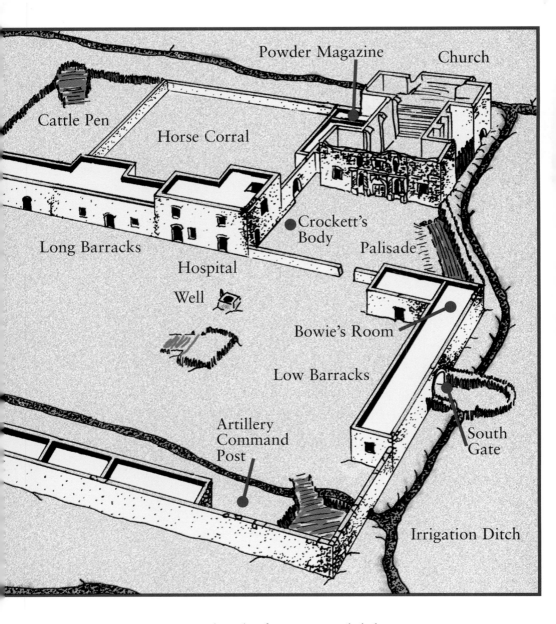

Powder Magazine

Church

Cattle Pen

Horse Corral

Crockett's Body

Palisade

Long Barracks

Hospital

Well

Bowie's Room

Low Barracks

Artillery Command Post

South Gate

Irrigation Ditch

Susanna asked if we could bury our loved ones.

The Mexican officer told us Santa Anna didn't want the men to be buried. He said, "The general ordered that all these bodies be burned."

43

When I heard this, a big lump formed in my throat. I was so angry. I couldn't speak.

I couldn't even cry anymore. Not to allow a fallen soldier to be buried was a great insult.

Santa Anna ordered that all the survivors of the battle be brought to him. I stood in front of him. And I held my head high. Susanna did too.

General Santa Anna was a small man. His uniform had much gold decoration. It seemed to glisten. A great, glittering sword dangled at his side. He paced back and forth. He waved his hands and shouted.

Santa Anna spoke to Susanna. He wanted her to take a message to Sam Houston.

"Tell General Houston that he cannot win this war," Santa Anna said.

"Tell him what happened at the Alamo. Also tell him it will happen to anyone foolish enough to fight me!"

Susanna and I were given horses to ride. We started out for the city of Gonzales.

That's where General Houston was. Susanna held Angelina on her lap.

We hadn't gone very far when it started to rain. We were soon soaked to the skin. Our clothes were caked with mud.

Two of Sam Houston's scouts found us on the road. They took us to the general.

Sam Houston was a big man. He had a booming voice. He had done many interesting things in his life. Besides being governor of Tennessee, he'd been a scout, a soldier, and a United States congressman.

Mr. Houston had even lived for a while with an American Indian tribe. He wore buckskin. He had a feather in his broad-brimmed hat.

We told him what had happened at the Alamo. He became very angry. He said he was determined to beat Santa Anna!

General Houston said the leaders of Texas had met at a town called Washington-on-the-Brazos. They had declared Texas an independent country. It was to be called the Republic of Texas!

The Alamo had fallen 46 days ago. Now Sam Houston's army had found Santa Anna's army.

General Houston had 800 men. Santa Anna had 1,500 men. The Mexican soldiers were resting at the top of a hill. Santa Anna was taking a nap under a tree!

Mr. Houston and his soldiers charged up the hill. The Texans shouted, "Remember the Alamo!"

Mr. Houston's men fought fiercely. The battle lasted only 18 minutes. When it was over, Santa Anna had been completely defeated. He had to promise to take his army out of Texas and never come back.

The battle was fought near the San Jacinto River. It was called the Battle of San Jacinto. At that battle, the free nation of Texas was really born!

The Republic of Texas elected Sam Houston as its first president.

Texas remained an independent country until 1845. Then it voted to join the United States of America.

I lived with Susanna and Angelina until I got married. Susanna married again too.

But no matter where our lives took us, Susanna and I never forgot what happened on March 6, 1836. We never forgot all the brave men who died on that day.

But we weren't the only ones who remembered. Wherever and whenever people fight for freedom and liberty, they call out "Remember the Alamo!"

THE ALAMO TODAY

CHAPTER NINE

THE REPUBLIC OF Texas gave the Alamo back to the Catholic Church.

In 1847, the church rented the Alamo to the United States Army. It was used to store weapons and medical supplies.

The army put a new roof on the chapel. They also added a rounded hump with two long windows to the top of the Long Barracks. That is how the Alamo still looks today.

In 1876, a man named Honore Grenet bought the Alamo from the church. He built a general store in the plaza. He also built a meat market, a restaurant, and a warehouse.

This upset many people in Texas. They didn't think such an important place in Texas history should be used in that way.

In 1905, Clara Driscoll bought the Alamo. Her grandfather had fought with Sam Houston at the Battle of San Jacinto. She gave the Alamo to the state of Texas.

The state gave the care of the Alamo to an organization called The Daughters of the Republic of Texas. Clara Driscoll was a member of this organization.

The Daughters of the Republic of Texas were very proud of the men who had died at the Alamo. They promised the state they would maintain the Alamo in "good order and repair."

In 1960, the Alamo was named a national historical landmark by the United States government.

If you take a trip to the Alamo, you can walk through the Long Barracks. It has been turned into a museum. This museum tells the story of the Battle of the Alamo. You can also visit a library there. References tell the four centuries of Texas history.

In the very center of the plaza, the Daughters of the Republic of Texas built a **shrine**. It is a memorial to the men who died fighting for freedom and for Texas. It helps us all "Remember the Alamo."

Glossary

adobe   brick made out of sun-dried earth and straw

barracks   lodging for soldiers

cantina   restaurant or saloon

fandango   dance or party

mission   local church or parish that depends on a religious organization for support

missionary   person who goes to a foreign land to teach a religion to the native people

plaza   public square or garden

pneumonia   disease of the lungs

sacristy   room in a church where sacred vessels and vestments (clothes) are kept. This is also where the clergy dresses before religious services.

serape	woolen blanket
senora	married woman
shrine	monument that shows great respect for the honored person or people
tortilla	round, thin cake made of cornmeal

REMEMBER THE ALAMO!